CONNECTICUT

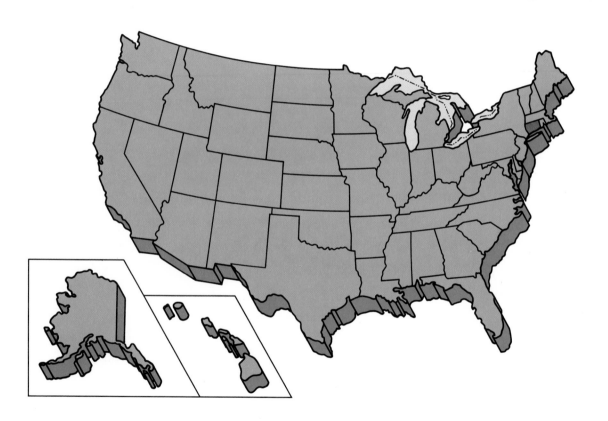

CONNECTICUT

Amy Gelman

 Lerner Publications Company

LIBRARY OF CONGRESS
CATALOGING-IN-PUBLICATION DATA
Gelman, Amy.
    Connecticut / Amy Gelman.
      p. cm. — (Hello USA)
    Includes index.
    Summary: Introduces the geography, history, people, industries, and other highlights of Connecticut.
    ISBN 0-8225-2709-X (lib. bdg.)
    1. Connecticut—Juvenile literature.
    [1. Connecticut.] I. Title. II. Series.
    F94.3.G45 1991
    974.6—dc20   90–13530
                            CIP
                            AC

Manufactured in the United States of America

1 2 3 4 5 6 7 8 9 10 99 98 97 96 95 94 93 92 91

Cover photograph by Thomas P. Benincas, Jr.

The glossary that begins on page 68 gives definitions of words shown in **bold type** in the text.

This book is printed on acid-free, recyclable paper.

Contents

Did You Know . . . ?

☐ Connecticuters must have quite a sweet tooth. The world's first lollipop was made by the Bradley-Smith Company in New Haven, Connecticut, in 1908. Other candies created in the state include Mounds and Pez.

☐ Connecticut is the only state in the country that has an official state hero. Nathan Hale, born and raised in Coventry, Connecticut, was a spy for General George Washington in the American War of Independence. Hale was caught by British soldiers and hanged in 1776. Connecticut adopted him as its official hero in 1985.

❏ One of the best places in the world to see ancient dinosaur tracks is Dinosaur State Park in Rocky Hill, Connecticut.

❏ Stone mined in Connecticut has been used in many buildings around the country and even farther away. Buckingham Palace, the home of the British royal family in London, England, has a piece of Connecticut.

❏ Connecticut is the third smallest state in the country—only Rhode Island and Delaware are smaller. Connecticut is so small, in fact, that it would fit into Alaska, the largest state, more than 117 times!

Visitors to Dinosaur State Park make plaster molds of dinosaur tracks.

A Trip Around the State

Connecticut is a tiny state—one of the smallest in the nation. The state often surprises visitors, who wonder how such a small place can offer so many different landscapes. Scenery around the state varies from forests and rolling hills to lush farmland and sparkling beaches.

Connecticut is the southernmost state in New England, a name that refers to the northeastern corner of the United States. Rhode Island lies to Connecticut's east, and Massachusetts is its neighbor to the north. New York borders Connecticut to the west, and Long Island Sound (an inlet of the Atlantic Ocean) forms the state's southern border.

Events that happened long ago helped shape Connecticut's landscape. Over 200 million years ago, volcanic lava flowed up from inside the earth and spread over central Connecticut. The lava hardened into ridges of solid rock, which still rise out of parts of central and eastern Connecticut.

More recently, perhaps 30,000 years ago, solid sheets of ice called **glaciers** covered what is now the northeastern United States. As these glaciers melted, they too changed Connecticut's terrain. The glaciers dragged piles of soil, rocks, and pebbles along the ground, making hills and ridges throughout the state. The melting ice filled hollow areas, creating many lakes and streams.

Most of the hills formed by the glaciers are in two regions, the Western Upland and the Eastern Upland, at either end of the state. The flatter Central Lowland region lies in between. In the southern part of the state, the narrow Coastal Lowland runs the length of Long Island Sound.

Connecticut's highest peaks tower over the Western Upland. The southern slope of Mount Frissell, the highest point in the state, rises to 2,380 feet (725 meters) in the northeastern corner of the region. Much of the Western Upland is still **rural**, with few big cities.

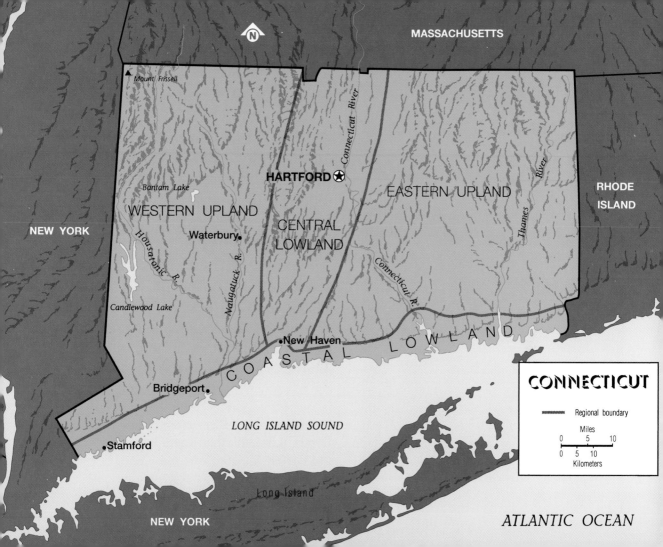

N

MASSACHUSETTS

▲ Mount Frissell

Bantam Lake

WESTERN UPLAND

Waterbury

Housatonic R.

Naugatuck R.

Candlewood Lake

HARTFORD ★

CENTRAL LOWLAND

Connecticut River

EASTERN UPLAND

Thames River

RHODE ISLAND

NEW YORK

Connecticut R.

New Haven

COASTAL LOWLAND

Bridgeport

Stamford

LONG ISLAND SOUND

Long Island

NEW YORK

ATLANTIC OCEAN

CONNECTICUT

〰〰〰 Regional boundary

Miles
0   5   10

0   5   10
Kilometers

The Central Lowland, which boasts Connecticut's best farmland, covers the central part of the state. Green, fertile valleys and wide ridges of volcanic rock make up the region's landscape. The long Connecticut River flows through much of the Central Lowland. Hartford, the state capital, lies on the western side of the river.

The hills of the Eastern Upland are lower than those in the Western Upland, and dense forests cover much of the area. Gently sloping hills and broad rock ridges alternate with fields and valleys.

The Connecticut River crosses the Central Lowland, then veers into the Eastern Upland, where it empties into Long Island Sound.

The Coastal Lowland, lower and flatter than the rest of the state, runs along the southernmost edge of Connecticut. The region claims several of Connecticut's largest cities. Sandy beaches cover the southern part of the Coastal Lowland. Many people who live in this region travel to nearby New York City to work.

The Connecticut is the state's major river. Many Indian tribes once made their homes on the river's banks, and early white settlers built the state's first towns there. Its name (and the state's) comes from an Indian word, *quinnihtukqut,* meaning "at the long tidal river." The Housatonic, the Naugatuck, and the Thames are other important rivers.

Connecticuters enjoy boating and swimming at a beach in the Coastal Lowland region.

13

Over a thousand lakes dot the Connecticut countryside. The largest of these is Lake Candlewood. An artificial lake, Candlewood was created when a **dam**, or barrier, was built across the Housatonic River. Construction workers dug a hole to store the water blocked off by the dam, and this stored water became Lake Candlewood. Glaciers carved out Bantam Lake, the state's largest natural lake.

14

. . . but winter can be cold
and snowy.

Weather in Connecticut—as any Connecticuter will tell you—can be unpredictable and often varies quite a bit from one part of the state to another. Temperatures are generally coolest in the upland hills and warmest in the lowlands. Winter temperatures in Connecticut average between 25° and 30° F (−4° and −1° C). Summer temperatures usually range between 68° and 72° F (20° and 22° C).

15

Beavers and other small mammals are easy to spot in Connecticut.

Connecticut has a lot of people for such a small state. They have crowded out most of the large animals, such as bears and panthers, that once prowled throughout the state.

Many small furry creatures, including rabbits, beavers, minks, and squirrels, still roam the state's fields and forests. A few fishers, small mammals that are cousins of the weasel, can be seen there too. White-tailed deer and a few moose occasionally dart through the woods.

Forests of ash, beech, birch, and oak cover much of Connecticut. Flowering mountain laurel bushes, which decorate hills and roadsides all over the state, are a familiar sight to people traveling through Connecticut's colorful landscape.

You're likely to see a black-capped chickadee like the one above in Connecticut's countryside. Mountain laurel *(right)*, the state flower, is another common sight.

17

The first Indians to live in Connecticut built houses called wigwams from saplings and large sheets of bark.

Connecticut's Story

Long before the first Europeans arrived in what is now Connecticut, hundreds of American Indian groups lived all over the area. Among them were the Niantic, the Podunk, and the Nipmuc. These people hunted animals and gathered wild plants for food in Connecticut's dense forests. They fished in its waters. Later, their descendants grew crops such as corn and tobacco.

The Indians cut trails across the land and made travel possible around the region. Many of the different Indian tribes could communicate with each other because they spoke closely related languages. These groups often traded with each other. A tribe living near a river, for example, might have traded fish to a tribe from a wooded area and gotten venison in exchange.

In the late 1500s, people from the Pequot nation moved into what is now Connecticut. The Pequot, whose name is said to mean "destroyers of men," quickly became the most powerful Native American group in the region. They took over control of some of the land from other tribes.

At about the same time, many Europeans were exploring North America. The first European known to have reached Connecticut was a Dutch explorer, Adriaen Block. He sailed up the Connecticut River in 1610, hoping to set up trade between the Indians and the Dutch. When he returned home, he described with enthusiasm the land he had seen, telling people about its great beauty.

Block's reports led a number of people from the Netherlands to move to the Connecticut River valley. These people settled near what is now Hartford.

Their settlement became part of the Dutch **colony** of New Netherland, a large area controlled by the government of the Netherlands, which was thousands of miles away. The colony included parts of modern New York, New Jersey, and Delaware as well as part of Connecticut.

The Dutch settlers bought land from the Pequot and traded with many local Indian groups. The newcomers exchanged European goods, including guns and alcohol, for seeds, crops, lumber, and animal furs.

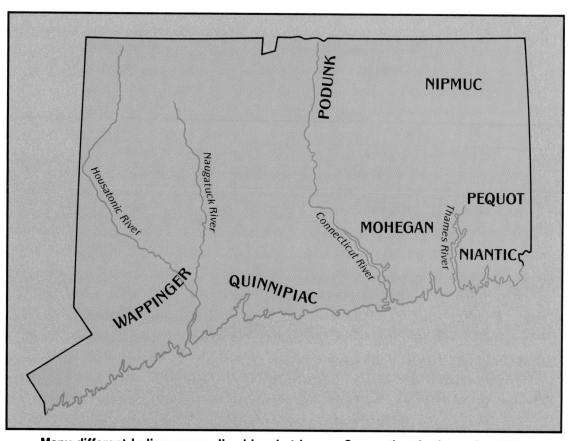

Many different Indian groups lived in what is now Connecticut in the early 1600s.

As the Dutch were settling in, people from the nearby Massachusetts Bay Colony were also exploring the fertile Connecticut River valley. They were **Puritans**—believers in a strict form of Christianity—who had left their home in Great Britain because they were not permitted to practice their religion there. As Massachusetts Bay became too crowded, some Puritans headed south.

The newcomers settled in and around three towns (later named Windsor, Wethersfield, and Hartford) on the Connecticut River. The towns formed the colony of Connecticut. Like other British settlers in nearby colonies, the Puritans of Connecticut followed the orders of the British government.

In 1638 more Puritans came to the region from Massachusetts Bay. They felt that the people of the Massachusetts Bay Colony weren't religious enough. They formed another colony, called New Haven, near Long Island Sound.

In 1638 Reverend Thomas Hooker led Puritans from the Massachusetts Bay Colony to settle in what is now Connecticut.

At first, the members of the two Puritan colonies lived in peace with their Indian neighbors. The colonists traded with local tribes, who taught the settlers to grow crops such as corn and beans.

As more European settlers came to the colonies, Native Americans willingly sold much of their land to the colonists. But the Indians believed that no one truly owned the land. They were sure that the colonists would let them keep using the land even after they had sold it.

The Europeans, however, did not share this attitude. As the settlers'

Connecticut's first church still stands in the town of Windsor.

Hartford's first settlers, including Reverend Thomas Hooker, are buried in this graveyard in Hartford.

demands for land increased, the Indians found they had less and less land. Where were they to hunt and grow crops? The relationship between Europeans and Indians became tense. The Pequot, who wanted more land to use, were especially unhappy with the colonists.

Violence soon broke out between the Pequot and the settlers. No one is sure which side began the fighting, but the Pequot and Puritans attacked each other several times during 1636. Finally, in 1637, Captain John Mason and his troops carried out one of the most terrible Indian massacres in American history. Mason's forces burned the main Pequot village, killing about 600 people in all.

The once-powerful Pequot were almost completely destroyed. The smaller Indian groups that remained were unable to stop the white people from taking over Indian land.

Many of the Indians who remained were killed in other battles, such as King Philip's War. This war was named after the tribal leader Metacomet, called King Philip by the whites. Hundreds of other Indians died of diseases they caught from the Europeans.

By the middle of the 1600s, most of the people in the colonies of Connecticut and New Haven were white people of British origin. A few hundred black Africans had been brought to the colony of Connecticut as slaves in the early 1600s. The Dutch, who were outnumbered by the British, had given up all claim to their settlements in the region.

Although white settlers were still under British rule, they wanted to set up a local government to take care of day-to-day business in the colonies. The leaders of the Connecticut Colony drafted the Fundamental Orders of 1639, which some people believe influenced the writing of the U.S. Constitution. The Fundamental Orders gave people the right to elect their own governor.

In 1662 King Charles II of Britain granted a Connecticut charter, which replaced the Fundamental Orders. The charter set boundaries for the region and required that the Connecticut and New Haven colonies be combined into one under the name of Connecticut.

In the late 1700s, the British government decided to take more control of all 13 of its North American colonies. It placed high

Opposite page: **The Connecticut charter, granted to the colony of Connecticut by King Charles II in 1662, gave the colony some independence from British rule.**

taxes on everyday items such as sugar and tea. The colonists felt that these taxes were unfair.

One of the most resented of the new taxes was the Stamp Act. This tax forced the colonists to pay for special stamps that the British government required on all newspapers, legal documents, and other printed materials.

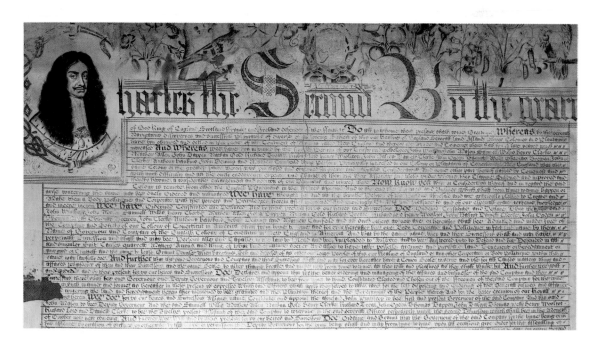

The government of Connecticut accepted the stamp tax, but many of its citizens did not. Some of them (including Jonathan Trumbull, who later became governor of the colony) formed a group called the Sons of Liberty to oppose the new British taxes.

The Sons of Liberty refused to use British goods. When a high tax was placed on tea, for example, the Sons of Liberty and their followers gave up tea and drank coffee instead.

One of the ways in which the British government tried to regain control of its colonies was to take back their charters. Connecticuters refused to give theirs up, and, to keep it safe, they hid it in an old oak tree—the Charter Oak in Hartford. The Charter Oak is no longer standing, but a monument (left) marks the place where the great tree once stood.

Modern-day Connecticuters act out a battle from the American War of Independence at Fort Griswold.

These actions, and similar protests in the other American colonies, eventually forced the British to cancel almost all of the taxes. But the colonists still resented British control and decided to break away. They prepared to fight for their independence.

The first battles between British and American troops broke out in Massachusetts in April 1775. More than 3,000 men from Connecticut rushed to Massachusetts to join in the fighting. The battles quickly led to a full-fledged war, the American War of Independence.

Connecticuters supported the American cause in many ways. The colony's farmers provided crops and cattle for hungry American troops. Manufacturers made guns and ammunition. The colony provided so much help for the army that people began to call it the Provisions State.

In the summer of 1776, representatives from each of the 13 American colonies signed the Declaration of Independence. This document declared freedom from British rule for the 13 colonies.

The dream of independence became a reality when the British surrendered in 1782. The American War of Independence officially ended the following year, and the United States was born. In 1788 Connecticut proudly joined the new nation as its fifth state.

As the 1800s began, **Yankees** (as the descendants of New England's Puritans were often called) in Connecticut gained a reputation for being clever and hardworking. At that time, many people went to work in the factories that manufacturers were building along the Connecticut and other rivers.

Water surging through dams on the state's many waterways turned huge engines that created electricity. This form of energy, called **hydropower,** was an inexpensive source of the electrical power needed to run machines at the state's factories.

As goods made in Connecticut became popular, many Connecticuters traveled to other states to sell their wares. Yankee peddlers became well known around the country.

Land of Steady Habits

In addition to high-quality goods, Connecticut has long been known for its many insurance companies. The first insurance company in the state was formed in 1795. A Hartford company sold the nation's first accident insurance, which protected a local businessman on the short walk to and from his office.

People and businesses pay insurance companies to protect them and their possessions in case of emergencies. For example, you can buy health insurance so that if you break your leg while playing sports, the insurance company will help pay your doctor's bill. Other common forms of insurance include accident and theft insurance for cars and fire insurance for homes and businesses.

Connecticut's insurance companies have a reputation for always paying what they promise. They have earned the state an unofficial nickname—the Land of Steady Habits.

By 1987 nearly 100 insurance companies had made their home in the state —about half of them in Hartford. In fact, Hartford is sometimes called the Insurance City.

The Travelers Insurance
Company, which has
offices in the Travelers
Tower in Hartford, is
one of many insurance
companies based in
Connecticut.

Guns and ammunition had been made in Connecticut since colonial times. But in the 1800s, workers in the state's cities began to make clocks, ships, hats, carriages, tinware, and cotton, silk, and wool cloth (textiles). In smaller towns, products such as inkstands and buttons were made.

The Civil War, which was fought between the Northern and Southern states, broke out in 1861. Many Connecticuters were willing to join the Northern side in the fight against slavery. Like other Northerners, most Connecticuters opposed slavery, which their state had outlawed in 1848. Connecticuters once again supplied guns and ammunition as well as soldiers.

The North won the Civil War in 1865, and slaves in the South were freed. Some former slaves moved north and settled in Connecticut. Around the same time, a small number of **immigrants** (newcomers) from Europe, mostly from Ireland, also settled in Connecticut. But by 1900, most people in the state were still Yankees whose families had lived in Connecticut for hundreds of years.

Colt's Firearms Company of Hartford

The famous Colt pistol was used all over the United States, but it was invented in Connecticut. Samuel Colt's gun-making factory in Hartford turned out many high-quality guns, such as the Texas Arm *(above),* which was used in the Mexican-American War (1846–1848). Colt invented the first handgun that could be fired several times in a row without stopping. Colt pistols were also widely used in the Civil War (1861–1865), and later in many famous shoot-outs in the American West.

Soon many more immigrants began to move into the state, this time mostly from Italy and eastern Europe. In fact, so many Europeans came to Connecticut that by 1930 only about one-third of its citizens were white Americans with American-born parents.

In the early 1930s, the Great Depression nearly destroyed the country's economy. In Connecticut, many factories and other businesses closed. Native Connecticuters and new immigrants alike lost their jobs, and poverty was widespread.

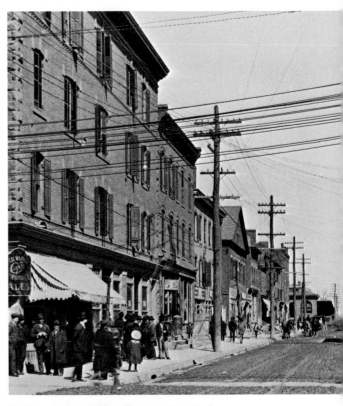

In the early 1900s, Connecticut's immigrants stuck together in ethnic neighborhoods in Hartford and other cities.

38

A modern skyscraper in New Haven reflects Connecticut's mixture of the new and the old.

When the United States entered World War II in 1941, Connecticuters once again helped supply the armed forces with guns, ammunition, and soldiers. Many people who had been out of work were able to find jobs in factories producing these goods. Connecticut's economy, along with the rest of the country's, quickly improved.

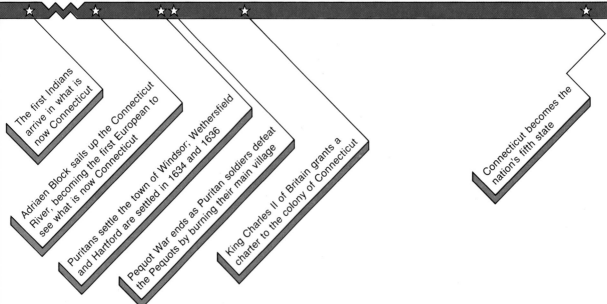

20,000 B.C.   **A.D. 1610**   **1633 1637**   **1662**   **1788**

The first Indians arrive in what is now Connecticut

Adriaen Block sails up the Connecticut River, becoming the first European to see what is now Connecticut

Puritans settle the town of Windsor; Wethersfield and Hartford are settled in 1634 and 1636

Pequot War ends as Puritan soldiers defeat the Pequots by burning their main village

King Charles II of Britain grants a charter to the colony of Connecticut

Connecticut becomes the nation's fifth state

Connecticuters are still known for their hard work and inventiveness. Their state is prosperous, and most Connecticuters have jobs. The descendants of the state's first settlers, Indian and Yankee, take great pride in Connecticut's history, and the many other ethnic groups in the state share that pride.

40

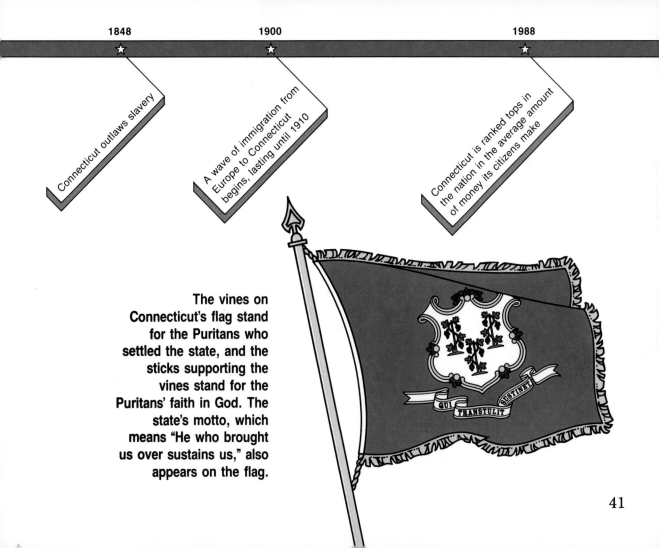

1848

Connecticut outlaws slavery

1900

A wave of immigration from Europe to Connecticut begins, lasting until 1910

1988

Connecticut is ranked tops in the nation in the average amount of money its citizens make

The vines on Connecticut's flag stand for the Puritans who settled the state, and the sticks supporting the vines stand for the Puritans' faith in God. The state's motto, which means "He who brought us over sustains us," also appears on the flag.

QUI TRANSTULIT SUSTINET

41

Connecticut offers both
bustling cities and
quiet countryside.

42

Living and Working in Connecticut

Much has changed in Connecticut since the first Europeans arrived. Perhaps the most noticeable change has been in the state's landscape. The countryside in which the Indians made their home hasn't disappeared, but alongside it are lively, bustling cities and suburbs. Much of the land in Connecticut is covered with forests, but homes, businesses, roads, and other signs of human activity are widespread too.

More than three million people live in Connecticut. That's a huge number for such a small state. Connecticut has about four times as many people as Montana—even though Montana is almost 30 times larger than Connecticut.

Most people in Connecticut live in **urban** areas (cities and suburbs), but small, uncrowded towns can still be found in the countryside. In fact, people often move to Connecticut because it offers many peaceful little towns that are not too far from the convenience and excitement of big cities such as Boston and New York.

People who live in Connecticut trace their origins to many different parts of the world. This is a change from the state's Yankee days, when most residents were British or Native American. Most modern-day Connecticuters were born in the United States. Many of them are descended from the immigrants who came to the state during the 1800s and 1900s.

Italian Americans make up the state's largest ethnic group, followed by people of Irish and British origin. Descendants of Poles, Germans, and French people are among other large groups.

In recent years, a new wave of immigrants, including blacks from Haiti, Hispanics from Central America, and Asians from Vietnam, have settled in Connecticut. Blacks, who have lived in Connecticut since colonial times, make up the fourth largest group in the state.

About 4,000 Native Americans, including members of tribes native to Connecticut, live in the state. The state runs five Indian reservations in Connecticut, but only about 175 Native Americans live on them. Other Native Americans, many of whom are only part Indian, live in cities and towns throughout the state.

Irish Americans celebrate St. Patrick's Day at a parade in New Haven.

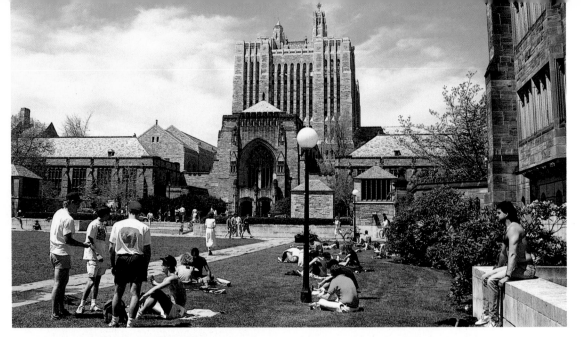

Yale University in New Haven is one of the most respected colleges in the country.

Connecticut has long been known for high-quality education. One of the best-known colleges in the country, Yale University, is found in New Haven, Connecticut.

The state can also claim the nation's first school devoted to teaching only law—Tapping Reeve Law School in Litchfield.

Not all Connecticuters have

46

A notice announces the opening of Prudence Crandall's school in Canterbury for young black women.

PRUDENCE CRANDALL,
PRINCIPAL OF THE CANTERBURY, (CONN.) FEMALE
BOARDING SCHOOL.

RETURNS her most sincere thanks to those who have patronized her School, and would give information that on the first Monday of April next, her School will be opened for the reception of young Ladies and little Misses of color. The branches taught are as follows:—Reading, Writing, Arithmetic, English Grammar, Geography, History, Natural and Moral Philosophy, Chemistry, Astronomy, Drawing and Painting, Music on the Piano, together with the French language.

☞The terms, including board, washing, and tuition, are $25 per quarter, one half paid in advance.

☞Books and Stationary will be furnished on the most reasonable terms.

For information respecting the School, reference may be made to the following gentlemen, viz.—

ARTHUR TAPPAN, Esq.
Rev. PETER WILLIAMS,
Rev. THEODORE RAYMOND
Rev. THEODORE WRIGHT, } N. YORK CITY.
Rev. SAMUEL C. CORNISH,
Rev. GEORGE BOURNE.
Rev. Mr. HAYBORN.

Mr. JAMES FORTEN. } PHILADELPHIA.
Mr. JOSEPH CASSEY,

Rev. S. J. MAY,—BROOKLYN, CT.
Rev. Mr BEMAN,—MIDDLETOWN, CT.
Rev. S. S. JOCELYN,—NEW-HAVEN, CT.
Wm. LLOYD GARRISON } BOSTON, MASS.
ARNOLD BUFFUM,
GEORGE BENSON.—PROVIDENCE, R. I.

always been able to go to school. In 1833 educator Prudence Crandall opened a school in Canterbury for young black women. Shortly after the school opened, however, angry white townspeople forced the school to close. Although most Connecticuters believed that blacks should not be slaves, not all of them wanted blacks to have the same rights as whites.

Arts and culture thrive in Connecticut, and the state boasts an unusual variety of museums. These range from the P. T. Barnum Museum in Bridgeport, which features exhibits from Barnum's famous circuses, to the renowned Peabody Museum of Natural History at Yale University.

Connecticut is an important center for regional theaters. Perhaps the best known of these is the Long Wharf Theatre, where many plays are first performed before

The P. T. Barnum Museum in Bridgeport displays the clothes that Tom Thumb wore in Barnum's circuses.

Fly fishing is a popular sporting activity in Connecticut.

they go on to larger audiences in New York City. Many notable writers, drawn to the state's peaceful beauty, live in Connecticut. Children's author and illustrator Maurice Sendak of Ridgefield is one of these.

Hockey fans in Connecticut turn out to root for the Hartford Whalers, Connecticut's only professional sports team. College teams such as the University of Connecticut's basketball team, the Connecticut Huskies, also draw their share of fans.

Most employed people in Connecticut (more than half of the state's workers) work in service jobs ranging from nursing to selling houses. The person who drives the train has a service job, and so does the cashier at the grocery store. In Connecticut, however, the best-known service is probably the **insurance** industry, which protects people and their property.

This worker puts together the parts of a jet engine at a factory in East Hartford.

Manufacturing is another leading industry in Connecticut. Nearly one-third of the money earned in the state comes from manufacturing, which employs about one out of four Connecticuters.

Instead of the hats, clocks, and ships for which Connecticut's manufacturers were once known, the state's workers now turn out modern items such as submarines, electrical and computer equipment, engines and propellers for jet airplanes, and parts for other machines. Pez candy and Lego toys are also among the goods made by Connecticuters.

Two workers prepare baked treats at the Pepperidge Farm plant in Norwalk.

A farmer from the Connecticut River valley sells some of his crops at a farmer's market in Hartford.

Most Connecticuters were farmers when the state was first settled. Agriculture became less important in the 1800s, when land became scarce and many people went to work in factories. Nonetheless, Connecticuters still run more than 3,500 farms. They produce goods such as eggs, milk, and tobacco, which provide a small part of the state's income.

Stone mined from quarries in Connecticut's Central Lowland region was used in many buildings in the 1800s and early 1900s. Crushed stone from the region is still used for paving roads and making concrete. Mining of this stone adds a small amount to the total money earned in the state.

Tourism also adds to Connecticut's earnings. In the summer, some tourists sunbathe, sail, and swim on Long Island Sound. Others fish in the state's waters. In the fall, people flock to rural Connecticut to admire the changing colors of autumn leaves. Throughout the year, tourists enjoy the activities that Connecticut offers. Tourists bring over two million dollars into the state each year.

Protecting the Environment

In the late 1980s, Connecticut's waterways made the news as gallons of waste leaked into Long Island Sound. Many fish and shellfish were killed, along with birds living in the marshes near the shore. Swimming was forbidden at many beaches.

This news caused great concern to many Connecticuters. Their state's numerous rivers, lakes, and streams, and Long Island Sound along its southern coast, have been important to the region since the first inhabitants arrived. The mighty Connecticut River was the site of many early settlements, both Indian and white.

Garbage is one of the many sources of Connecticut's water pollution.

Sewage sometimes leaks into the water from sewage treatment plants.

The abundance of water in Connecticut, along with the lack of much fertile land, helped the state's industries to develop in the 1800s. Machine shops, textile mills, and factories were built on the state's waters, where they could use hydropower as a source of energy.

While Connecticut's industries have helped keep the state's economy strong, they have also contributed to pollution in the state's waters. Over the years, many factories have poured chemicals and wastes into the rivers and streams of the state. These chemicals are usually poisonous to the fish and other creatures that live in and near the waters.

The state's large and growing human population has also added to the pollution problem. People create **sewage**, which moves with water through sinks, toilets, and other fixtures that humans use. Water that contains sewage is called **wastewater.**

Solids, oil, and some other pollutants are usually removed from wastewater at treatment plants before it is released into the state's water supply. But treated wastewater still contains some pollutants that cause damage to waterways.

Much greater damage is done if sewage leaks into waterways before it has been treated. Raw sewage makes water unsafe to drink or use for cooking or washing. Raw sewage leaks are what forced the beach closings of the late 1980s.

Lawn and Garden: Chemicals such as fertilizers and pesticides wash off lawns when it rains, and the rainwater carries these pollutants to the nearest storm sewer. Watering the lawn or garden too heavily can also add pollutants to wastewater.

WHERE WASTEWATER COMES FROM

Wastewater comes from sinks, toilets, baths and showers, and even lawns and gardens. It travels through sewers and eventually ends up in waterways.

Bathroom: Waste and water from toilets, sinks, showers, and baths add to the wastewater that goes through sewage treatment plants.

Storm Sewer

Kitchen: Kitchen cleaning products and soapy water from dishwashers and washing machines are emptied into drains that go to sewage treatment plants. Eventually, the wastewater enters waterways.

Car: Cars drip oil and other chemicals onto roads and driveways. These pollutants drain into storm sewers — underground pipes that empty into waterways. Used motor oil poured on the road will also end up in a nearby waterway. Even the cleaners used to wash a car add to wastewater pollution.

Rainwater that carries pollutants is also called wastewater. Rainwater brings pollutants to **storm sewers,** underground pipes that empty into Connecticut's waterways. These pollutants come from many sources, such as landfills where garbage is buried, and even from lawns and gardens, where people spread chemicals to help plants grow.

Connecticut's government has taken steps to make its waters cleaner. It passed a law forbidding most industries to pour chemicals directly into waterways. If companies don't obey this rule, the government makes them pay for each fish they kill in Connecticut's waters.

59

Some individuals are trying to help control water pollution, too. A group of commercial fishermen, for example, patrols Long Island Sound to make sure that sewage plants don't dump raw sewage into the water.

Connecticuters who are worried about their state's water can take other steps to prevent pollution. Using less water at home can help avoid leaks at sewage treatment plants, which usually occur when the plants are overloaded with sewage. Even turning off the water while brushing teeth can make a difference.

Because of the efforts of Connecticut's government and people, rivers such as the Connecticut are the cleanest they have been since the 1800s. Many rivers and streams that were once badly polluted are

These oyster beds have been polluted by wastewater from a treatment plant downstream.

Connecticuters help keep their state beautiful by cleaning up trash on the beaches of Long Island Sound.

becoming safe again for fish and for swimmers. With continued concern and care, Connecticut can continue to offer the beauty and variety that have drawn people to it for centuries.

Connecticut's Famous People

ACTIVISTS

John Brown (1800–1859) was a famous opponent of slavery. Before the Civil War outlawed slavery in America, Brown helped slaves escape to Canada, where they could be free. He also led a group of men to battle in Kansas to keep Kansas from allowing slavery. Brown was born in Torrington, Connecticut.

Ralph Nader (born 1934), from Winsted, Connecticut, is well known for his efforts to protect people from products that are unsafe. Since the 1960s, he has been calling attention to problems with certain cars, chemicals, and other goods to make people aware of the possible dangers of using these products.

JOHN ▲
BROWN

KATHARINE ▶
HEPBURN

ACTORS

Katharine Hepburn (born 1909) has had a long and successful career as an actress. She has won four Academy Awards for her acting — more than anyone in the history of movies. Hepburn was born in Hartford, Connecticut.

Paul Newman (born 1925) has been a popular movie actor for many years. He studied acting at the Yale Drama School in New Haven, Connecticut, and has lived in Westport, Connecticut, since the early 1960s. He also owns a food company, Newman's Own, that donates all of its profits to charity.

▲ IVAN LENDL

◀ PAUL
NEWMAN

ATHLETES

Ivan Lendl (born 1960) is a tennis champion. Lendl was born in Czechoslovakia, but has lived in Greenwich, Connecticut, since the 1980s. He has won many tournaments and has been ranked as the top player in men's tennis for much of his career.

Calvin Murphy (born 1948) holds two National Basketball Association (NBA) records for his free-throw shooting. Murphy began playing basketball at Norwalk High School in Norwalk, Connecticut. He played professionally for the San Diego Rockets (who later moved to Houston) of the NBA.

◄ CALVIN MURPHY

◄ CHARLES HENRY DOW

▲ J. P. MORGAN

◄ ELLA GRASSO

BUSINESS LEADERS

Charles Henry Dow (1851–1902), born in Sterling, Connecticut, was a financier (a type of businessman). With Edward D. Jones, he founded the *Wall Street Journal*, a daily business newspaper. Dow and Jones also created the Dow-Jones average, which gives people information about the stock market.

John Pierpont (J. P.) Morgan (1837–1913) was a financier. He founded the U.S. Steel Corporation, the first company in the world to be worth $1 billion. He was born in Hartford, Connecticut.

POLITICIANS & LEADERS

Ella T. Grasso (1919–1981), born in Windsor Locks, Connecticut, was the first woman in the United States to be elected governor in her own right. (Earlier female governors had taken over the office from their husbands after their husbands had died.) After holding various state and national offices, Grasso became governor in 1975 and stayed in office until 1980.

63

Adam Clayton Powell, Jr. (1908–1972), was a member of the U.S. Congress from 1944 to 1970. For much of his career, he was one of only two blacks in Congress. He was also a pastor of the Baptist church. Although he lived in New York for most of his life, Powell was born in New Haven, Connecticut.

Uncas (1588?–1683?) was born a Pequot Indian of Connecticut, but led some of his people to form a new tribe called the Mohegans. The Mohegans fought on the side of the British colonists during the Pequot War, and after the Pequots were defeated, Uncas became the leader of the surviving Pequots.

◀ ADAM C. POWELL, JR.

AARON LERNER ▶

▲ BONNIE TIBURZI

ELI WHITNEY ▶

SCIENTISTS & ACHIEVERS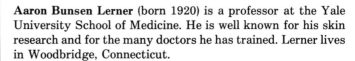

Aaron Bunsen Lerner (born 1920) is a professor at the Yale University School of Medicine. He is well known for his skin research and for the many doctors he has trained. Lerner lives in Woodbridge, Connecticut.

Bonnie Tiburzi (born 1950) is an airline pilot from Danbury, Connecticut. In 1973, she became the first woman to be hired as a pilot by a major airline.

Eli Whitney (1765–1825) of New Haven, Connecticut, invented a method of making goods that was put to use all over the world. The method, known as mass production, made it possible to put goods together much more quickly than they could be made by hand. Whitney's other inventions include the cotton gin, a machine that pulls fibers off of cotton seeds.

64

TRAITOR

Benedict Arnold (1741–1801), born in Norwich, Connecticut, was a respected officer of the American army in the American War of Independence. In the middle of the war, however, he turned traitor and joined the British forces. His name has become part of our language—to say someone is a Benedict Arnold means that person is a traitor.

◀ BENEDICT
ARNOLD

SAMUEL CLEMENS ▲
and family

WRITERS

Samuel Clemens (1835–1910), better known as Mark Twain, was a great American author. Among his most popular books are *The Adventures of Tom Sawyer* and *Adventures of Huckleberry Finn.* A native of Missouri, Twain lived in Hartford, Connecticut, from 1871 to 1891 and wrote some of his most famous books there.

Maurice Sendak (born 1928) is an author and illustrator of children's books. He started his career as a comic-book artist. Perhaps his best-loved book is *Where the Wild Things Are.* Sendak lives in Ridgefield, Connecticut.

Noah Webster (1758–1843) was a lexicographer (a person who makes dictionaries). He was also a lawyer, teacher, and journalist. Webster, born in West Hartford, Connecticut, began publishing dictionaries in 1806. Revised versions of *Webster's Dictionary* are still widely used.

65

Facts-at-a-Glance

Nickname: Constitution State
Song: "Yankee Doodle"
Motto: *Qui Transtulit Sustinet*
  (He Who Brought Us Over Sustains Us)
Flower: mountain laurel
Tree: white oak
Bird: American robin
Hero: Nathan Hale

Population: 3,279,000 (1990 estimate)
Rank in population, nationwide: 28th
Area: 5,018 sq m (12,997 sq km)
Rank in area, nationwide: 48th
Date & ranking of statehood:
  January 9, 1788, the 5th state
Capital: Hartford
Major cities (and populations*):
  Bridgeport (141,980), Hartford (137,980), New
  Haven (123,450), Waterbury (102,300), Stam-
  ford (101,080)
U.S. senators: 2
U.S. representatives: 6
Electoral votes: 8

Places to visit: P. T. Barnum Museum in Bridge-
port, Dinosaur State Park in Rocky Hill, Indian Burial
Grounds in Norwich, Peabody Museum of Natural
History at Yale University in New Haven, Mystic
Marinelife Aquarium in Mystic

Annual events: Lobster Festival in Mystic (May),
Barnum Festival in Bridgeport (June), Italian Festival
in Middletown (Sept.), Noah Webster Birthday Par-
ty in West Hartford (Sept.), Apple Harvest Festival
in Glastonbury (Oct.)

* 1986 estimates

66

Average January temperature: 26° F (–3° C)   **Average July temperature:** 71° F (22° C)

Natural resources: soil, stone, sand, gravel, clay, water

Agricultural products: eggs, milk, greenhouse and nursery products, tobacco

Manufactured goods: transportation equipment (including jet engines and submarines), machinery, metal, rubber and plastic products, chemicals, primary metals, printed materials, food products

ENDANGERED SPECIES
Mammals—least shrew, northern flying squirrel, fisher, eastern cougar, deer mouse
Birds—snowy egret, least tern, American oyster-catcher, piping plover
Reptiles—bog turtle, five-lined skink, slimy sala-mander, timber rattlesnake
Fish—Atlantic sturgeon, slimy sculpin
Plants—marsh horsetail, fir club moss, showy lady-slipper, panic grass, Indian paintbrush

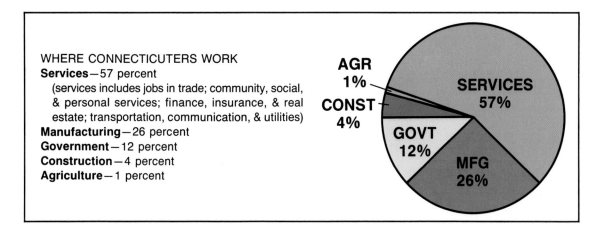

WHERE CONNECTICUTERS WORK
Services—57 percent
  (services includes jobs in trade; community, social, & personal services; finance, insurance, & real estate; transportation, communication, & utilities)
Manufacturing—26 percent
Government—12 percent
Construction—4 percent
Agriculture—1 percent

AGR 1%
CONST 4%
SERVICES 57%
GOVT 12%
MFG 26%

PRONUNCIATION GUIDE

Connecticut (kuh-NEHD-uh-kuht)

Block, Adriaen (BLAHK, AY-dree-uhn)

Frissell, Mount (frih-ZELL, mownt)

Housatonic (hoo-suh-TAHN-ihk)

Massachusetts (mass-uh-CHOO-suhts)

Naugatuck (NAW-guh-tuhk)

Niantic (ny-AN-tihk)

Pequot (PEE-kwaht)

Podunk (POH-duhngk)

Thames (TEHMZ)

Wappinger (WAH-pihn-jur)

colony A territory ruled by a country some distance away.

dam A barrier built to control the flow of water in a river, or a body of water held back by a barrier.

glacier A large body of ice and snow that moves slowly over land.

hydropower The electricity produced by using waterpower. Also called hydro-electric power.

immigrant A person who moves into a foreign country and settles there.

insurance The protection of people or their possessions against damage or loss.

68

Puritan   A member of an English religious group that followed a strict form of Christianity. Many Puritans left Great Britain during the 1600s because they were not allowed to practice their religion there.

rural   Having to do with the countryside or farming.

sewage   Wastewater that travels through pipes from buildings, usually to a treatment plant.

storm sewer   An underground pipe that carries rainwater and other materials to waterways.

urban   Having to do with cities and large towns.

wastewater   Water that carries waste, or sewage, from homes, businesses, and industries.

Yankee   A resident of New England, especially someone descended from the area's Puritan settlers.

69

Index

Acknowledgments:

Thomas P. Benincas, Jr., pp. 2–3, 13, 15, 39, 42 (left and right), 45, 46, 53, 69; Maryland Cartographics, Inc., pp. 2, 11; © 1991 Sallie G. Sprague, p. 7; Betty Groskin (photo agent: Jeff Greenberg), p. 8; Connecticut Valley Tourism Commission, p. 12; Jeff Greenberg, p. 14; © John D. Cunningham / Visuals Unlimited, p. 16; Paul Fusco, Connecticut DEP Wildlife Division, pp. 17 (left), 55; Monica V. Brown, Photographic Artist, p. 17 (right); Greater Hartford Convention and Visitors Bureau, pp. 18, 25, 52, 71; Laura Westlund, pp. 21, 41; Library of Congress, pp. 23, 33, 37 (top left), p. 62 (top right), p. 63 (middle right), p. 64 (bottom left); Elizabeth Bray Wilkens, p. 24; Rare Books and Manuscripts Division, The New York Public Library, Astor, Lenox, and Tilden Foundations, p. 26; State Archives, Connecticut State Library, Picture Group 220, Box 3 (photo by Gus Johnson), p. 29; James Mejuto Photo, p. 30; Southeastern Connecticut Tourism Division, p. 31; The Travelers, p. 35; Wadsworth Atheneum, p. 37 (bottom left); Connecticut Historical Society, p. 38 (detail); Prudence Crandall Museum, Canterbury, Connecticut, administered by the Connecticut Historical Commission, p. 47; The Barnum Museum, p. 48; Farmington Valley / West Hartford Visitors Bureau, p. 49; Pratt and Whitney, p. 50; Pepperidge Farm, p. 51; John Dommers, Connecticut Coastal Program Staff, p. 56; Dale Redpath, pp. 58–59; Runk / Schoenberger from Grant Heilman, p. 60; Schooner Inc., p. 61; Hollywood Book & Poster Co., p. 62 (bottom left, top right); Spectrum Sports, p. 62 (bottom right); Dow Jones & Company, p. 63 (middle left); American Airlines, p. 63 (bottom left); The Houston Rockets, p. 63 (top right); Independent Picture Service, p. 64 (top left and right), p. 65 (top right); Mark Twain Memorial, p. 65 (bottom left).